Always Everly

Nate Wragg

HARPER

An Imprint of HarperCollinsPublishers

ISBN 978-0-06-298279-7

The artist used acrylic paint and paper collage to create the illustrations for this book.
Typography by Chelsea C. Donaldson
21 22 23 24 25   RTLO   10 9 8 7 6 5 4 3 2 1
❖
First Edition

For Crystal and Willow—
thank you for your endless seasons
of love and inspiration.

It was spring when a small tree sprouted up at the edge of the woods.

Her name was **Everly.**

Hello.

Even though she was new,

she quickly made friends—

and fit in perfectly.

Until, one day,
everyone began to change—
everyone except for Everly.

She hoped no one noticed. . . .

But they did. Everly's friends
looked so beautiful, so colorful.
As for Everly, she just looked different.

And she felt different too.

She wished she could look like everyone else.

One morning it seemed
her wish had come true!

Unfortunately, it was just a false alarm.

She did what she could to blend in,

but that didn't work either.

Everly tried everything she could think of.
Perhaps a little extra sun would help.

Or a little shade?

Would extra watering do the trick?

No, nothing worked. Everly had run out of ideas.

But not me. I just wish I could be like all of you.

Everly realized that being different
was a good thing. She was so
overjoyed, she began to glow . . .

. . . in her own **PERFECT** way!